The ARTIST WHO LOVED CATS

The Inspiring Tale of Théophile-Alexandre Steinlen

words by Susan Schaefer Bernardo • pictures by Courtenay Fletcher

Inner Flower Child Books

LOS ANGELES

As she was strolling down the Rue Montcalm,
with a fresh baguette tucked under her arm,
Antoinette paused to see what was new
in the cluttered shop window of Monsieur Arvieux.

There were lots of things she had seen already:

a broken old clock and that one-eyed teddy,

The sign said open, so she pushed on the door,
which made a bell tinkle at the back of the store,

which made Monsieur Arvieux come down the stair
and up to the front to see who was there.

porcelain dolls and a china dish,

leather-bound books and a filigree fish,

candelabra and a silver ladle

and twenty-three goblets on a spindly table.

She peered deeper inside...and her eyes opened WIDE!
"I don't recall that interesting cat.
I wonder where Monsieur found that?"

"Bonjour, Antoinette!" he said with a smile.
"Have you time to come in and browse for a while?"

"Bonjour," she replied.
"Comment allez-vous?"
(That's French for "Good day"
and "How do you do?")

"Please, will you tell me
about that sweet little cat?"
And she pointed to the shelf
where the little cat sat.

"Oh...the bronze? It's by Steinlen! That's one of his cats!
It's really quite rare..."

"Steinlen? Who's that?"

Monsieur was soon holding the cat in his hand,
so she dropped the baguette in an umbrella stand
and set herself down on a comfortable stool,
because Monsieur's tales were the best kind of school!

"Théophile Steinlen was an artist, of course,
who loved to observe and draw cats of all sorts."

"Ooooh," said Antoniette.
"Please tell me more.
I love to hear stories
about things in your store!"

"Excusez–moi," said the cat, "this is my tale to tell!
I knew Monsieur Steinlen. I knew him quite well."

"Hmmmmm," purred Noir.
"Where shall I start?
How does an artist
begin to make art?"

When Steinlen was young, even younger than you,
he started to draw, and he drew and he drew.
He loved to watch cats tumble and play
and spent hours sketching us every which way.

In school, Steinlen studied fabric design,
worked hard, got a job and was doing just fine.

Still...

He wanted to paint! He wanted to draw
all of the interesting things that he saw!

He wasn't enticed by cathedrals or kings,
preferred everyday people doing everyday things.
He drew laundresses and farmers and women in hats,
but most of all, Steinlen still loved to draw cats.

In 1881, Steinlen moved with his wife
to Paris to embrace the creative life.

Oh, what a time
to arrive in this city!
The culture, the characters –
so wild! So witty!
And on the edge of Paris
at the top of a hill
lay Montmartre with its art
and its busy windmills.

Here the feet of every woman and man
marched to the beat of we-can-can-can-can!
We can do what it takes to follow our heart!
We can make the world better with our music and art!

Fifty-six cats (and nary a mouse)
lived with his family in a sweet little house.

Steinlen had talent –
he was willing and able,
but at first, it was hard
to put food on the table.

After hours drawing scenes
that he saw on the street,
he traded his sketches
for something to eat.

He met friends at Chat Noir, that chic cabaret
known for lively salons and unique shadow plays.
It was such an inspiring place to be,
rubbing shoulders with Ravel, Valadon, and Satie!

The cabarets were bustling with many musicians who needed cool covers for their compositions, and Chat Noir began printing its own magazine full of stories and songs from the cabaret scene.

Steinlen was asked to submit illustrations.
At first he accepted with some hesitation.
(Have you ever been nervous to try something new?
Not sure it was something you'd be able to do?)
Steinlen gave it a try and was glad he said yes,
because his cartoons of cats were a surprising success.

In posters, he featured his daughter Colette,
or his pets (like you see in this ad for a vet).
He drew bicycles, cocoa and soldiers in hats,
but most of all, Steinlen still loved to draw cats.

Steinlen's sketches protested the cruelties of war,
revealed injustice and the plight of the poor.
He didn't use fists or weapons or words,
instead he chose art to make his voice heard.

Pencil and ink,

pastel and crayon...

Théophile Steinlen

was a versatile man.

He captured the sights

that he saw on his walks

with etching and sketching,

charcoal and chalks

and just a few little sculptures,

like the one you see here.

That's the reason this cat

is so precious, my dear.

Monsieur placed the cat on its shelf, retrieved the baguette
and walked to the door, saying, "Au revoir, Antoinette!
This world is abounding with magic and mystery!
Each thing has a past. Each place has a history!
You can make the world better with music and art,
if you keep your eyes open and follow your heart."

"Mais oui, but of course! I shall always do that!
Be curious and creative, like artists – and cats."
"Au revoir," she added, "et merci, chers messieurs."
(That's French for "goodbye and thank you, dear sirs.")

Théophile-Alexandre
Steinlen

1859 ~ 1923

Steinlen? Who's That?

Théophile-Alexandre Steinlen was born in Lausanne, Switzerland in 1859. At his father's urging, he studied textile design in college, so that he would have a practical way to make a living. In 1881, Steinlen decided to pursue his dream of being a fine artist and moved to Montmartre, a lively village on the fringe of Paris that attracted many artists, writers and musicians. There he met Rodolphe Salis, a fellow Swiss, who had founded a cabaret (a place where people gathered to enjoy meals, entertainment and lively conversation). The cabaret was called "Le Chat Noir" – The Black Cat.

Salis asked Steinlen to submit illustrations to the cabaret's new magazine and also hired him to create posters to advertise Le Chat Noir. In time, Steinlen became a prolific, successful illustrator, fine artist and graphic designer, producing more than 700 illustrations for journals, as well as songbook covers, storybooks, paintings, posters and sculptures. His work influenced many other artists including Pablo Picasso. Steinlen also used his art to protest social injustice and war and to celebrate the lives of working people.

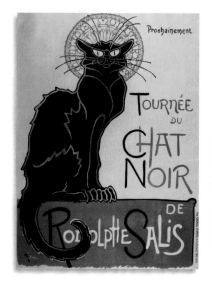

1896

Steinlen's "Le Chat Noir" poster, commissioned in 1896, is a beloved symbol of Montmartre's cabaret scene. Why do you think it became famous?

1895

1896

1899

1905

Did you notice these posters on pages 22 and 23?
They are Steinlen's original advertising posters.

Each Thing Has a Past, Each Place Has a History

This book began when the author took a stroll through Montmartre in the summer of 2014 and fell in love with a little bronze cat in the shop window of Antiquités Montcalm. That little cat now lives in California with the author and her family. Antiques and artifacts can intrigue and inspire us hundreds, even thousands, of years after their creation. They make us wonder about the world as it was – how people lived and worked, what they thought and dreamed and did.

Can you find these items from Monsieur Arvieux's antique store being used elsewhere in the book, as they might have been used during Steinlen's lifetime?

They Made the World Better with Their Music & Art

Jane Avril
· DANCER ·

People from the past inspire us, too! Montmartre was an exciting place to live in the late 1800s. It still is today. In 1881, the French government passed a law that allowed new freedom of the press, and Montmartre became a hub for creativity and expression.

Did you find these famous people who rubbed shoulders with Steinlen in the cabarets and on the lively streets of Montmartre?

Erik Satie
· COMPOSER·

Toulouse-Lautrec
·ARTIST·

Suzanne Valadon
· PAINTER·

Maurice Ravel
· COMPOSER·

Yvette Guilbert
· SINGER·

Tilly & Hattie

Pandora

Edward & Isabella

Silvie

Love and thanks to the people
and furry friends who helped
make this project purr.
Et merci beaucoup to
Monsieur Steinlen and the
City of Lights for inspiring
creative souls everywhere.
~ xoxo Courtenay & Susan

Mouse
& Newman

Berkley

Text copyright ©2019 by Susan Schaefer Bernardo
Illustrations copyright ©2019 by Courtenay Fletcher

First Edition: June 2019
10 9 8 7 6 5 4 3 2 1
ISBN 978-0971122888 (hardcover)

Library of Congress Control Number: 2018909931

Visit us at www.InnerFlowerChild.com
Book design by Courtenay Fletcher.
Printed and bound in the USA by Bang Printing.

Rosie

Publisher's Cataloging-In-Publication Data (Prepared by The Donohue Group, Inc.)
Names: Bernardo, Susan Schaefer, author. | Fletcher, Courtenay, illustrator.
Title: The artist who loved cats : the inspiring tale of Théophile-Alexandre Steinlen / words,
        Susan Schaefer Bernardo ; pictures, Courtenay Fletcher.
Description: First edition. | [Los Angeles, California] : Inner Flower Child Books, 2019. |
        Interest age level: 005-008. |
Summary: A fictional biography of Théophile Alexandre Steinlen, the French artist who
        is famous for the Le Chat Noir cabaret posters. Many of Steinlen's artworks
        featured cats, his favorite subject.
Identifiers: ISBN 9780971122888 (hardcover) | ISBN 9780971122871 (ebook)
Subjects: LCSH: Steinlen, Théophile Alexandre, 1859-1923--Juvenile fiction. | Artists--
        France--Paris--History--19th century--Juvenile fiction. | Cats in art--Juvenile fiction. |
        CYAC: Steinlen, Théophile Alexandre, 1859-1923--Fiction. | Artists--France--Paris--
        History--19th century--Fiction. | Cats in art--Fiction. | LCGFT: Biographical fiction.
Classification: LCC PZ7.B47 Ar 2019 (print) | LCC PZ7.B47 (ebook) | DDC [E]--dc23

SUSTAINABLE
FORESTRY
INITIATIVE

Certified Chain of Custody
Promoting Sustainable Forestry
www.sfiprogram.org
SFI-01268

SFI label applies to the text stock

We love trees!